O9-BTO-230

Now gather round kids,
this here is the story of . . .

For those who love them some Halloween!

SIMON & SCHUSTER BOOKS FOR YOUNG READERS
An imprint of Simon & Schuster Children's Publishing Division
1230 Avenue of the Americas, New York, New York 10020
Copyright © 2010 by Rhode Montijo

For information about special discounts for bulk purchases, please contact
Simon & Schuster Special Sales at 1-866-506-1949 or business@simonandschuster.com.
The Simon & Schuster Speakers Bureau can bring authors to your live event.
For more information or to book an event,
contact the Simon & Schuster Speakers Bureau at
1-866-248-3049 or visit our website at www.simonspeakers.com.

Book design by Laurent Linn
The text for this book is set in Providence Sans.
The illustrations for this book are rendered in brush and ink, then colored digitally.
Manufactured in China
1109 SCP
2 4 6 8 10 9 7 5 3 1

CIP data for this book is available from the Library of Congress.
ISBN 978-1-4169-3575-9

first
edition

THE HALLOWEEN KID

Rhode Montijo

SIMON & SCHUSTER BOOKS FOR YOUNG READERS

NEW YORK   LONDON   TORONTO   SYDNEY

Halloween is usually a time for good ol'-fashioned dressin' up and gettin' some sweet eats.

But sometimes there are more
tricks than treats.
Like the time them Toilet Paper
Mummies rolled into town!

When trouble like this happened,
folks would call on . . .

the Halloween Kid!

You see, the Halloween Kid loved
him some Halloween and he would
wrangle those who tried to ruin it.
He'd swoop down on his trusty steed
and *sweep up creeps.*

Nobody knew who the Halloween
Kid was, or where he came from.
All they knew was that he wasn't
afraid of nothin'!

He wrassled pumpkin-suckin' vampires.

And some say he even took down the Giant Miami Werewolf!

... just one more step, you woolly williker.

Ooh-wee, that Halloween Kid was good!

In fact, he done did such a good job
at wranglin' Halloween hoodlums, that
Halloween was just dandy for years.

That is, until the year Goodie Goblins
showed up runnin' loose and stealin'
sweets like there was no tomorrow!

Some folks locked their doors and
kept their li'l younguns inside.

And some folks started handin'
out things that wasn't even candy.
It was horrible!

But it got worse . . .
folks started talkin' 'bout
cancelin' Halloween for good.

Hearin' that bad news done did it for the Halloween Kid. He showed up lickety-split!

Them Goodie Goblins scattered quick-
like, and the Halloween Kid only caught
one of 'em. Being gone so long had made
his wranglin' a bit rusty. He didn't give
up though, because he had trackin' skills.

The Halloween Kid found gooey
Goodie Goblin tracks and followed
them to a cave out in the woods.
He went inside.

And then somethin' happened that never had before . . . the Halloween Kid was ambushed!

Luckily, his horse got away and hightailed it back to town.

"Look, it's the Halloween Kid's horse!" said one trick-or-treater.

"Where's the Halloween Kid?" asked another.

"What is it, boy? Is there some sort of trouble?"

"This is horrible. What are we going to do?" asked one.

"We have to go help him!" said another.

"But I'm scared."

"Me t-t-too, but the Halloween Kid always helped us when there was trouble, now *he's* in trouble."

"You're right!"

"Let's go!"

When they got there, they found them Goodie Goblins dog-piled on top of the Halloween Kid!

Suddenly the Goblins stopped.
Was that candy they smelled?

Them Goodie Goblins just couldn't resist!

The Halloween Kid hopped up in a hurry
and leaped on his horse.

Then them Goodie Goblins got a-runnin.'

and nabbed every last one of 'em!
Everyone cheered.

"How can we ever thank you?"
they asked the Halloween Kid.

"Thank me? I couldn't have roped
them rascals without your help,
pardners. Y'all showing up when you
did made all the difference. Them
Goodie Goblins never stood a chance.

"Y'all keep trick-or-treatin' now,
ya hear?" and with a wink, he rode
into the moonlit sky.